AF090748

MO(A)T
Stories from Arabic

Mo(a)t:
Stories from Arabic

First published in this edition by UEA Publishing Project 2021
Editorial copyright © Garen J. Torikian 2021
International © 2021 retained by individual authors and artists.

The right of Garen J. Torikian to be identified as the Editor and Sawad Hussain and Nariman Youssef as the translators of this work has been asserted by them in accordance with the with the Copyright, Design & Patents Act, 1988.
Design and typesetting by Anna Brewster
Typeset in Adobe Garamond
Printed by Imprint Digital
Distributed by Ingram / NBN International

This book is sold subject to the condition that it shall not, by way of trade or otherwise, be lent, resold, hired out, stored in a retrieval system, or otherwise circulated without the publisher's prior consent in any form of binding or cover other than that in which it is published and without a similar condition including this condition being imposed on the subsequent purchaser.

All stories originally published in Arabic as follows:

Najwa Binshatwan's two stories were published in a collection titled *An Going Coincidence* in 2019 by Riad El-Rayyes Books in Beirut.
Dr. Ishraga Mustafa Hamid's stories were published in 2016 by Sefsafa in Giza.
Mariem Hamoud's story "My Father Died Twice" was published on March 2020 by Al-Bayan Magazine. "Still Running" was published in a previous collection on October 2019 by Melad House in the Kingdom of Saudi Arabia. "The Truth Is Not Enough" was published on July 2020 by Nizwa magazine.
Ahmed Isselmou's stories were published in 2015 by Arab Scientific Publishers in Beirut.
Batoul Mahjoub's novel "Minefields" was published in 2016 by Dar Fadaat in Amman.
Arthur Gabriel Yak's stories were published in a collection titled *Gabo Danes Flamenco and Tango* in 2018 by Rafiki Publishing House in Juba.

ISBN 978-1-913861-19-3

Introduction

An introduction is a difficult thing to write, all the more so when what you're trying to introduce is a concept so well-defined in the imagination, but which has no easy transformation into words. What you're about to read is a collection of contemporary fiction, originally written in Arabic and expertly translated by Sawad Hussain and Nariman Youssef. But the story behind these stories is more layered.

In 2019, I pursued a Masters in Literary Translation at the University of East Anglia, in Norwich. For a very long time, I had felt a calling to do *something* with Armenian literature. I knew that hundreds of years of Armenian literature sat untranslated, due to genocide and diasporic dispersion. As no one else was taking up the call, I decided to take seriously the responsibility of bringing these works to readers of English. I ended up writing my dissertation on an author named Zareh Vorpuni, a survivor of the Armenian genocide who emigrated to France. What I found most curious about him was the fact that, although he spoke French fluently, modelled his style after Proust, and moved amidst all the writerly circles of 1960s Paris, he chose to write fiction in Armenian. For him, it was not a matter of pride, but a matter of expression: French was the language he used to communicate with the world around him, but Armenian was the language he used to communicate his soul. I understood all too well what Vorpuni was doing. In a sense, to write in French would be the 'easier' option if one's goal for writing was to simply be published and read. But writing in Armenian was the more natural choice, at the expense of limiting one's audience.

The instruments which an artist uses to create their work is just as interesting as the end result. I became fascinated with trying to understand what it must feel like for a writer to move through the spaces around them, surrounded by words that are not one's own. There exists the well-documented process of exophony, where a writer writes in a language that is not their mother tongue—think of Beckett in French, or Yoko Tawada in German. I don't think that there's a concise phrasing for what I'm talking about, something of an inverse: a writer writing in their mother tongue, but living in a country where that language is not the predominant one. Hence, the idea of a moat emerged: I imagined a writer sitting in their castle, protected by their native language, and surveying the land. At any point, this writer may lower the drawbridge and engage with the community around them. The writer is not quite an island, but also not wholly immersed in their environs, either.

When I first approached Sawad and Nari to be the translators on this project, their first question was not 'Why are you making this?' but rather, 'Why Arabic?' Most of the time, an Arabic work would only find its way into translation if a publisher decided a superstar author would do well in English markets. I don't speak Arabic, and while this may have a whiff of cultural appropriation, I will follow up with the fact that my parents were born in Cairo, as the children of Armenian immigrants. In a sense, everything I've discussed above has happened to my family, twice. In Egypt, my family moved around in an Arabic world, but they spoke Armenian to each other. After they emigrated to America, we moved around in English, but our personal language remained Armenian. (Growing up, I was very aware of Arabic as the language my parents used when they didn't want the children to understand something; nonetheless, I can ululate with the best of them.)

However benign my relationship with Arabic is, it cannot be denied that for most of the rest of the world, speakers of Arabic have become the stereotypical personae non gratae, due to racist and ignorant policies. Yet Arabic literature also operates in a way that Armenian literature does not. There are less than ten million speakers of Armenian; there are hundreds of millions of Arabic speakers. Even with such a huge volume of literary content, there's still a severe lack of Arabic works available in English.

So much of immigration, translation, and publishing is based on chance, but those opportunities only come about after consciously acting on a long series of decisions. In 2019, I attended a workshop led by Sawad and Nari on translating Arabic comic books, and I kept in touch with them over the years. Further, this collection manifested from an idea into something tangible and real based on an elective I chose to take, innocuously titled 'Publishing: A Practical Approach'. For that, I must thank Jen McDerra. This book was initially workshopped (and encouraged) during her course. It is the final result of a year-long process to learn every aspect of the publishing industry, from sourcing material, budgeting expenditures, coordinating with writers and translators, communicating with designers, and working with printers.

What you hold in your hand is not only an experiment, but a manifestation of the dreams of many people. The stories in this anthology are not centred around a theme, but rather, a concept. Each author lives outside of their birth country—whether by choice or exile—yet in their writing, they choose to continue to express themselves in their mother tongue, rather than in the language of their adopted homes. *Mo(a)t* examines the consequences of a kind of literary 'nature versus nurture'. It explores how writers are influenced by the language they are immersed in, or whether they work to bring forth from themselves the stories which they carry in their souls. These authors are writing new and original stories in places where Arabic is relegated to a minority language; by bringing their stories into English, we hope to make their voices heard.

From Norwich, UK and Brooklyn, NY
May 2021

Translators' Notes

Cairo writes, Beirut publishes, Baghdad reads. It's been a while since the old maxim reflected the realities of Arabic literature. Yet, for many readers looking for stories from the Arab world, the idea that the hub is located somewhere on that stretch of the map with the Levant at its centre still persists.

An online literature festival that made history in 2020 as the first 'African language festival' featured Kiswahili, Hausa, Lingala, Ewe, IsiZulu, Amharic, Yoruba, and Shona—but no Arabic.

A survey of 'African literature' taught in universities worldwide gathered a list of 671 texts from respondents. On this list, Algeria, Morocco and Egypt are the only Arabic-speaking countries with ten or (slightly) more texts.

So where do the writers featured in this collection fall? Between the cracks. Neither Arab enough to be considered within the Arab literary tradition, nor African enough to be included in Africa-centred literary festivals. When Garen Torikian approached us with an idea for an anthology of writers whose experiences represent an in-betweenness of place, it seemed natural to reach for those whose in-betweenness is also one of language.

Having said this, the qualities that make this collection stand out aren't solely based on where the authors are from, but rather originate from the linguistic choices they have made, whether in dialogue with, or against the grain of, the language(s) shared by their milieu. The personal cadences, rhythm, and style of each writer may be influenced by linguistic worlds as starkly different as German and Arabic, or by the diaglossic richness of living between, say, Gulf Arabic and Mauritanian Arabic.

Above all, works written in Arabic from the African continent are what we are celebrating in this anthology. When curating the stories, we weren't looking for whether they were 'African' or 'Arab' enough.

The English-speaking literary ecosystem expects narratives from certain countries—where the literary output must surely be less, where every literary publication must surely be a triumph—to be performative. It assumes that a Mauritanian text will sell better if it explains Mauritanian culture, or that a Libyan text that delves into tribal history will resonate more with readers. If the works included in this anthology perform anything at all, it is simply good literature. They may be personal or political, fast-paced, comic, or lyrical. Ultimately, these stories exist in their own right and describe the world on their own terms, without catering to the expectations of a mythical reader about how they should sound or what they should explain, whether that reader is in the West or in the proverbial Baghdad.

From Cambridge and London, UK
May 2021

Contents

Najwa Binshatwan,
translated by Sawad Hussain

Portrait of a Libyan Scream	13
A Monotonous Transaction	20

Dr. Ishraga Mustafa Hamid,
translated by Nariman Youssef

We Have a River of Stone *To Virginia Woolf*	27
Vera Maria	30
Antonia	32

Mariem Hamoud,
translated by Nariman Youssef

My Father's Footsteps	35
My Father Died Twice	37
Still Running	40
The Truth Is Not Enough	42

Ahmed Isselmou,
translated by Sawad Hussain

Floating Paper 47

Hamidinou's Smile 50

Batoul Mahjoub,
translated by Nariman Youssef

Extract from *Minefields* 59

Arthur Gabriel Yak,
translated by Sawad Hussain

Divorce 67

A God and His People 70

Mama Regina's Cruel Blessing 72

**Najwa Binshatwan,
translated by Sawad Hussain**

Portrait of a Libyan Scream

The sole lamppost in the village decided to keel over onto Ikhmayyis' head while on his way home. Usually, no one could make their way home, or their way out of the village, without passing by the post. Not only was it munificent in lighting their path, day and night, but it also became, of its own accord, a traffic light, whenever it felt that a car was about to knock into it. Those who were lost found their way, thanks to said lamppost, and it also defended the village from locust storms, whilst providing much-needed shade from the unrelenting sun.

Ikhmayyis was neither annoyed nor upset with the historical lamppost's choice to fall on him. In fact, it was a privilege worthy of thanks, even if it made his glass eye pop out, cutting out both his sight and all electricity in the village in one fell swoop.

'A blessing in disguise. Ye may despise something while it is good for you,' Ikhmayyis murmured, reminding himself of the Quranic verse, whilst crawling on his hands and knees, groping here and there, left only with his feeble other eye, hoping to find his glass one. He replayed the scene in his mind. Either it sank into the sand, or rolled under the lamppost and shattered.

Possibly!

It was also possible that someone would find it and return it to him, though that wasn't what the villagers were known for, declaring it would bring them bad luck to do so.

Placing his palm on the cavity left behind on his face, he made his way back home, woebegone. From the window, his mother spotted him shielding half of his face and knew that her son had lost his eye, again. She rushed to the door with the platter of couscous she was carrying rather than making her way to the table, and yelled, agitated, 'What happened to you, unlucky lump? Lost your eye again?'

Thinking she had come to pour couscous over his head, Ikhmayyis stuck to the wall, shrieking as if electrocuted. His father came charging out with a cane, convinced his son needed to be disciplined; the household swirled, a maelstrom of sounds. Furniture smashing, doors slamming, howling. Neighbours stood at their windows, craning their necks, trying to make sense of the family commotion they were hearing.

As for the platter of couscous in Mama Ikhmayyis' hand, it tried to wriggle out, and push Baba Ikhmayyis away from his son with whatever heat it had left.

'Woooooh unto me, don't you dare hurt his other eye! On your mother's life, just leave his face alone,' Mama Ikhmayyis pleaded.

The CIA would probably surmise that the steaming couscous platter had played a pivotal role in breaking up the brawl by singeing Baba Ikhmayyis' paunch. Otherwise, they'd still be quarrelling today.

Ikhmayyis had always been anxious about being in a crowd with his glass eye, cupping his hands around it. He had always been cautious, considering what usually happened in a crowd, something or other being dropped: wallet, phone, keys, words, tongue, the colour from an outfit...

He had had his delicate glass eye for years. What would he do if he were to lose it? The factory that manufactured it had shuttered, declaring bankruptcy. Maintenance required travelling abroad. Travel required a lot of money. And a lot of money meant stealing. Stealing money might as well have been considered a real career. Everyone was doing it. How else was a person meant to get rich, even if they toiled from dawn to dusk?

The surface of Ikhmayyis' glass eye had been scuffed during his teenage years, when he couldn't stop leering at girls. As a young man, when harassing women, many times his eye had fallen out, creating nothing short of a public scandal. And so, everyone came to know why Ikhmayyis' eye would pop out, or why it would be dangling by his cheek if it didn't fall out completely. When the lamppost fell, it put an end to any such future embarrassments once and for all, folding this dark page from Ikhmayyis' life, leaving people's tongues wagging about the story of the radiant lamppost rather than of him. The blessed lamppost had saved Ikhmayyis from their sharp tongues, no matter whatever he had lost.

Ikhmayyis was forced to tolerate the biting morning cold penetrating his eye socket, standing in front of the garage, issuing optical licenses and permissions for new eyes in one of the city's old streets, a place where there were countless things that could infect his empty socket. Crud here and there, filthy restaurants, overflowing sewers, polluted air, cars that couldn't drive without spitting out black fumes. There stood Ikhmayyis, waiting for the arrival of the government official who had the keys to the license office.

Ikhmayyis spotted him standing at the falafel and beans eatery, ordering his usual. 'Hey you bayumi, Nile-boy, make it one bean sandwich with harissa, and two falafel. Don't forget my cold Pepsi.'

The official started to devour what the Egyptian server brought him, as if he had been in a famine, not simply a man who had just rolled out of bed. Unable to endure the cold any longer, Ikhmayyis went to ask for assistance. 'Good morning khuya.'

'Khuya? How am I *your* brother?' the official responded, his mouth stuffed with pieces of beans.

'Sorry, sorry, sorry. I mean, aren't you the esteemed official in charge of new eyes?'

'What do you want?' he snapped.

'My eye, my eye,' Ikhmayyis moaned, his hand placed where his eye should have been. 'I mean, my eye fell out and I need a new one.'

Ikhmayyis had made a mistake by interrupting the man's hot meal. The official shook, and roared, 'Can't you see that I'm busy?'

'Sorry, sorry! I can't see too well. Dig in, dig in.'

Ikhmayyis left the official to wipe his plate clean and yelled out to the server, 'Hey Nile-boy, two spoons of harissa for the big man here and a cold Pepsi on me.'

After an hour of beans, falafel, tea, talk of sports, politics, religion, the supernatural, and of course the Palestinian issue, the official moseyed on over to the garage. He sluggishly pulled the shutter upwards, as if he didn't see Ikhmayyis standing, waiting, frozen in place.

A man with a glass eye came forth from the furthest corner of the eatery, the smell of fresh glue wafting off him. He asked Ikhmayyis if there was work today or not.

'Ask the big man,' he responded, tears falling from his eye because of the bitter cold, and other things. 'I swear to God, I've been here since seven o'clock and still don't have a clue.'

The man was one of those nosey ones, his type having been around since the fourth century AH.

'Why are you here?' he asked Ikhmayyis.

'My eye, O, my eye,' Ikhmayyis groaned.

The man burst out laughing, as if Ikhmayyis had said something funny, then revealed the other half of his face. 'If this face gets an eye before you, you can have it! Look how I've had to keep gluing my eye back in because they never have new ones.'

The man had one cold eye and one hot eye. The cold one would focus on hot things, while the hot one would focus on cold things. In his youth, the man would help his mother heat up things and cool down others. Say for example, alleviating his brother's fever, heating up bath water in the wintertime, warming the clothes iron, cooling down what was left of the food, then heating it up. When prosperity and well-being set in the country, and the electricity was no longer cut off, clothes arrived ironed from the clothes line, food arrived cooked from the kitchen, and vegetables had merely to get to know each other before cooking themselves—the man's glass eye became unemployed and started to fall out, during prayer, or whilst playing football. And here he was in front of the garage of licenses—because of what prosperity had reduced him to.

Ikhmayyis nearly got frustrated, hearing this drawn-out history of the eye, but he postponed his blowout till later, waiting for the official to settle down in his chair, turn on the heating, the television, the three 350-watt bulbs, and finally light his cigarette.

'Tell me again, what do you want?' he finally asked Ikhmayyis, frowning, without looking at him.

'To get a new eye, kind sir. And a movement permit, please. May God bless you.'

The official let rip a cracking burp, bits of falafel and beans spewing out his nose. 'Well, getting a new eye is one thing, and getting the movement permit is another.'

'May God give you long life sir. Just give me whatever you have and I'll come back later for the rest.'

The official opened one of his drawers, sloth-like, fishing out a pen. It then occurred to him to turn on the computer. Ikhmayyis stole a glance at him, saying to himself, 'Ayeeeee! Now he'll start looking for a piece of paper, and stall even more!'

But the official didn't do any of that; he just sat contented with his pen. 'Getting a used eye has different requirements than getting a new eye.'

He started to tap on the keyboard, the pen between his fingers, throwing Ikhmayyis some questions before deciding his fate.

'For a used one, you need a certificate proving you have no priors, stamped of course, your family booklet, your national ID, four witnesses, and 500 dinars along with the application form. For a new one, in addition to all that, just 100 dinars from one hundred men in the tribe, and you will need to take a new driving test down at the traffic department, the vehicles section, and a certificate of weapons saying that you have passed the shooting test for pistols and long-range rifles.'

'But I haven't shot a gun in my life!'

The official laughed so hard, gas burst out his backside. Ikhmayyis cheeks grew hot. Then, calming down as his gas slowly faded, the official said, 'Deal with it, these are the regulations.'

'Can't you help me out with a used one?'

'Well, I do have one that some people gave me a while ago; their father died, they buried him without it. The daughters wanted to keep it as a memento, but the sons sold it to make some money and start their own business. It comes with strings attached you see.'

'Strings attached... No, no, I don't want any of that.'

The official opened another drawer and took out a can. He put his hand on top of it and started talking about it so sacredly he might as well have been swearing on the Quran.

'This is from someone who lost his eye in the war and afterwards was martyred. Allah yarhamu, his body hasn't been found, even to this day. A proud eye it is, you can walk with your head held high.'

17

Ikhmayyis had goosebumps all over. 'Yes, God rest his soul,' he stuttered. 'But, the eye of someone who died in a war? I've had one of those before and death is all I saw. I'm not a fighter. I'm a sensitive man, who works in a bakery, and only knows the fire of love and the fire of the oven. Give me something else, something less tragic, on your father's life, please.'

'Hold on, let me call one of my friends in Taykah.'

Taykah is the place that time forgot, thought Ikhmayyis to himself. 'His grandfather is just about to give up the ghost in a few days. A real treasure box he is; he's got gold and marble teeth, and a green glass eye. Each family member has taken their piece of him, for their own livelihood you know, afraid to even leave him in the hospital, because who knows what might be stolen from him there.'

'What if he takes too long to die and I'm just hanging around here?'

'BAH! There's no pleasing you it seems! What can I tell you? Hold on, I may have one in the trunk, it's been a while since I looked in there. I think I used it as an indicator at one point. Hold on, let me go check and see if it fits you.'

The official disappeared for a few moments, then came back with a plastic bag in hand. He took out the eye and blew off the dust from it, in several different directions, then wiped it with his sleeve before giving it to Ikhmayyis. Ikhmayyis popped it in, saying, 'Bismillah', then left to test drive it in front of the garage.

'So, what do you think? It's not that expensive,' the official said.

'I can see people clearly, and the whole street is very clear. But everything behind it is black, as if it wasn't day at all.'

The official got closer to the eye. He tried adjusting it, blew on it, wiped it.

'And now?'

'The background is still black.'

'Uff! You're just seeing the black life that we live. Here, here, give it back, give it back.'

Ikhmayyis took out the eye and threw it in the bag once more. And thus, it became necessary for Ikhmayyis to join one of the militias to get an eye test done for free. Sure, he needed to shoot a pistol, a rifle, a machine gun, and a cannon, but they would then determine the kind of eye that he needed, its size, the dimensions of vision, and everything related to the technical details that were required when aiming a bazooka.

Ikhmayyis' healthy eye jiggled in its socket; he had never handled a weapon before. It jiggled before all the weapons. He then felt it rolling down his cheek and fall out in front of him, leaving his face empty.

'O God, help me!'

His yell could be heard everywhere. It entered the Red Castle and left through one of the throats of the statues hidden there, then it entered one of the ears of the Libyan Venus statue, destroying love as an axe does a mirror. Ikhmayyis himself, left where he was for the coastal road, wandering, repeating, 'Are you all happy now? Are you all happy now? Even my good eye is gone now! Nothing's ever enough for you!'

From Ikhmayyis' eye socket the contents of his head slipped out, his memories spilling on the road, his ideas disordered, scattered everywhere, his secrets running among the sewers, mixing with the rainwater and the sewage on its way to the sea. It's even said that his scream can still be heard on the coastal road between Tripoli and Zawiya—the contentious road which is closed at times and open at others—till today.

Eye witnesses add that they saw Ikhmayyis' scream there, pulling at its head and wailing; the sheer intensity of his scream sending camels into cooking pots, men into the grave, making djinns visible, humans invisible, and all lampposts felled by the wayside.

A Monotonous Transaction

Abdul Samie didn't hear the rest of the phone call. What was said after 'We've got your wife' was as indecipherable as random dictionary entries extracted from the Lisan Al-Arab. Confused as he was, his brain still managed to draw a three-dimensional model of the Tawargha refugee camp in Benghazi, trying to pinpoint why his wife Fathia would have been kidnapped. Why take a poor woman living in a refugee camp? He scanned her body in his mind, trying to figure out which curve or Stygian cranny would tempt them to abduct her.

Untethered, his imagination galloped, his thoughts homing in on her legs. How different were they from Sheikh Khaled's beard, really? Ever since Fathia had been ousted from her home, she hadn't waxed. Did her abductors know the story of Fathia's displaced legs, and why they hadn't been waxed since the war broke out in Benghazi? It wasn't that Fathia was apathetic about her personal hygiene, God forbid. Or that she didn't take her spouse's carnal desires into consideration, but rather, ever since being displaced from her home in Tawargha, she had never had any privacy. Wherever she went, someone else was already there. In Benghazi, she sought refuge from one school building to the next; how could anyone live in such a disgraceful state—let alone have any privacy!

After having been displaced nearly a thousand kilometres from Tawargha to Benghazi, for standing with Gaddafi, it happened to her all over again in the capital. The Misrata militants and their allies started to hound them all, with rockets, rifles, mines; bombarding them with bullshit.

In the refugee camp, Fathia had left a tanjara of beans atop some firewood she had kindled, waiting for the Misrata folk showed some goodwill—meaning Fathia and those like her could go back home. But the Misrata folk were not forgiving in any sense, chasing Fathia and the others out of the camp, planting mines on all of the routes home, making sure to seize the pot and the beans.

This is how the doppelgänger to Sheikh Khaled's beard appeared in Benghazi schools, and how the twin of Fathia's legs appeared on national religious TV channels.

Abdel Samie's head vibrated atop his neck, as though he was

re-experiencing the final jolt of electricity he had received at General Tawargha Hospital, where he used to repair the morgue fridges. Fathia, abducted—how did it make any sense? Was this even possible? Where was their conscience? Wasn't it enough for them to know that she's from a godforsaken refugee camp?

Abdel Samie hurried to the fourth-grade classroom where his aunt, Fathia's mother, stayed, trying to get a hold of himself and the too-small flip flops he had on, to tell her that Fathia wouldn't be back today, and that her hairy legs were now the property of a gang, only to be seen again in exchange for an eye-watering amount of money.

During the rush between the classroom where he stayed and the one where his mother-in-law resided, kidnapping stories sprung to his mind, ones he had heard since becoming a refugee in his own country. One was about a man who kidnapped his relative—by mutual agreement—to bargain with their family for a ransom, which they would split and then invest in future projects. Then there was that wife who claimed that she had been kidnapped, but she really just ran off with her boyfriend. What did Fathia have to gain by being in cahoots with the kidnappers? All that he and Fathia owned was the rain from the sky, the cold of open spaces, and some onions.

Did this have something to do with the spat they had had the day before, over the money they had received through charity?

'Your wife went to sell harissa and cake, and you had no clue,' the devil, standing at the door of the sixth-grade classroom, told him.

'How dare she lie to me!'

'Yes, she's probably hiding some money from you too, for all you know,' the devil said, goading him. The space between Abdel Samie's eyebrows grew narrower, as if they were welded together.

'She better come back,' he said to the devil within. 'Or else.'

This last utterance entered his mother-in-law's classroom with him, so, surprised, she asked him, 'Who won't be back?'

'Fathia.'

'She doesn't have anywhere to go!' her mother lamented, not missing a beat.

Abdel Samie, or the devil within, responded, 'Well, seems like she's flown the coup, taken off with her lover!'

At this terrible news, the chalkboard promptly fell on the old woman's head and she wailed, tapping into an octave she hadn't used since her husband's demise. In less than a minute, all the chalkboards in the school had fallen off the walls.

'O, O, binti, what's happened to you?' The hole at the neckline of her robe ripped even further in her distress. The frozen equations written in chalk, overcome with emotion, peeled off the board, scattering here and there, like a sugar bomb over the lofty pyramid of knowledge instituted by the government.

As his mother-in-law wailed, her voice shattering hanging things one after the other in a sort of chain reaction, one of the kidnappers called Abdel Samie. It was clear from his voice that he had put a sock on the burner phone he was speaking from. Even if Libya was a country of no police, no justice, and no law, with no one caring to track criminals down to begin with, not even their own destiny, the thieves still took such precautionary measures. They demanded a ransom from Abdel Samie, refusing to listen to anything he had to say. All he managed to get out was, 'Her mother's old' and 'She has a new-born.'

They cut the call and then called again half an hour later. Abdel Samie thought that God had struck their hearts with mercy, but the devil told him to stop being so naïve. If God wanted to get involved, he could easily free Fathia directly instead of getting the scoundrels to shape up. Why should he help *them* on her account?

Abdel Samie, his mother-in-law, and some relatives from the other classrooms waited for the phone to ring, for the kidnappers to have pity. But the phone never rung on that long bitter Benghazi winter night, for the rains had ravaged the camp of the Tawarga refugees, drowning them.

All that was left of the family scene awaiting the call was Abdel Samie's too-small flip-flop, floating next to the metal tanjara which accompanied Fathia from one displacement to the next.

* * *

'Wallah, the villa isn't mine, I'm just the cleaner. The owner is in Egypt.' Fathia pleaded, her bones quivering before the unrelenting kidnappers.

'You own the villa and you're one of the Azlam, aren't you? You Gaddafi supporters, running from the west to here. Which means you're loaded, which means don't take us for fools you wily woman!'

The gang couldn't believe that Abdel Samie wasn't responding to their calls. They had no idea that his cellphone had drowned along with the camp. Instead, one of them thought that he was entertaining the idea of getting rid of his wife. People take advantage like that in such chaotic times.

The gang grew tired of the monotonous transaction; it had coincided with the dropping of missiles on the camp, intended for Al-Keesh square to break up the demonstrations. It became even thornier when a stray bullet from a wedding celebration nearby pierced Fathia's head as she prepared the kidnappers' meal. When she cried out for help, the devil goaded the kidnappers: 'You've got to do something—the woman is still alive.'

'Let's drop her off in the 1200-bed hospital.'

'What rotten luck we've got!'

'It's all your fault,' the youngest of the bunch piped up. 'You're the one who said we should go to the villa and then sat there talking strategy. We shouldn't have gotten so caught up in your plan.'

The deliberations about what to do with Fathia dragged on until she took her last breath in a place she didn't know, a place she hadn't come to as a displaced person or a runaway, but as an abductee. Her soul bid farewell to her child still in the camp and then went on its way to meet her maker. Her body was curled up in the middle of the kidnappers. They were drunk, hoping to forget their bad luck and their first failed criminal act.

Benghazi was drowning in fear, darkness, and criminality. The kidnappers used a tarp to transport the body and throw it in the hospital parking lot, but there was another woman's corpse already there. 'No, no, my children,' she said. 'No space here, not at all. Al-Zayt street is a better bet, no one will notice another corpse being dumped there.'

After the deal went south, the gang went back to square one, deciding to offer a favour to science by performing an autopsy on Fathia, for they were newly graduated medical students after all. Her good-for-nothing blood flowed over the hands of the kidnapper holding the knife, like the burnt oil of an engine. He said to his collaborator, 'Write boy, in the name of God, the heart is stringy, and the gallbladder full of pus. The skin has been dead for seven years and the stomach is split between the rice of alms and radioactive Ukrainian flour, and the liver has the following lyrics etched on it:

> *Time, your deeds are callous*
> *To withstand you takes prowess*
> *Every joy of mine is tarnished*
> *All my days in sorrow languished*

As for the breasts, they are full of skimmed milk—what a waste of time!'

Two of the newly-graduated doctors differed on the matter of her brain: one of them concluded that it was in pieces due to the stray bullet, while the other figured that the bullet was just the straw that broke the camel's back. She obviously had suffered blow after blow, loss after loss in her life, causing her brain to finally explode.

Fathia's final resting place was on Al-Zayt street, nestled against the body of a man giving her warmth, melting away the coldness of displacement, allowing her dead, neglected skin to feel the tingle of affection all over for the first time. It was an undeniable fact of death on Al-Zayt street: you got the chance to know the rest of the casualties, without the barriers of class, clan, or anything else.

Another body with torture marks slid over Fathia's, revealing the legs which would eventually help to identify her. Her face was no longer recognizable. It had changed too much. It became the face of prey, not that of a woman.

Dr. Ishraga Mustafa Hamid,
translated by Nariman Youssef

We Have a River of Stone
To Virginia Woolf

Here is the Viennese night, a night of longing and contemplation. The ink's tears can tell you about my rivers, waves, and stones.

I can tell you about a woman who came here carrying her wounds, her sorrows, her loves, disappointments, and great dreams. I can tell you of a burning coal I found once upon a mountain under the ashes of storytelling, a coal I hold tightly. It pains and illuminates my heart whenever the night of longing sharpens its teeth.

Your river is my mirror. My stories are its shimmer. Your river knows your secret and mine.

The time was the end of August in a year of the Years of the Ashes.

I was buried under the rubble. For nothing pains me more than the thanklessness and conforming masculinity of the heart. Nothing ever.

Don't sleep, Virginia. My story with you is only just beginning, here by the river.

Across that river of yours, I told you my story and learned the secrets of your depression.

What is depression? It is to find yourself, after a long tending towards the self, opening your generous heart and sprinkling it with salt and the pearls of your tears. It is to find an excuse for every scratch etched in your heart, every wound, every transgressor.

Depression is to bare yourself, until the flesh of light in your wound is revealed, then to walk the path of your heart, the path of your transparency, of your humanity, of a room with pens, papers, many books and a perfume bottle.

A room, Virginia! The room with the walls that protect us. Where I find shelter akin to a mother's tender embrace. I tell her my stories and she tells me hers. She gathers me into the folds of her mud. The faraway walls of Vienna's homes, the walls that told me stories of war and poverty and apple trees. A room to shelter our solitude.

Solitude is me. It's you. It's entering the cocoon of sweet loneliness and sitting with a lantern inside yourself that illuminates your sorrow and your need to scream, without being accused of madness.

This woman full of sorrows, who sits across from your soul, fills the place with the narrative of humanity. She believes in its consistency and contradictions. Every time life slaps her in the face, she responds with the anthems of defiance.

Oh Virginia, I fear for you as I tell you about life's bitter blows. And I'm no Jesus to turn the other cheek. I'm turning my cheek nowhere but to face the path before me.

I saw you raise the banner of your first idea. I saw you and my eyes widened with my passion for life.

I feel naked, the tree of my body without its bark.

Something was lost while I was combing the maze of dust looking for a safe grave that wouldn't be dug up by disloyal dogs.

I fear dogs and I know that your people adore them.

Dogs are loyal to their people, they say.

I am propped up by my people, my ashes returned to their mountain. The mountain *I* once was went into labour and delivered nothing but a mouse. The ashes are my personal legend, the legacy of my phoenix spirit. The ashes are a beautiful mouse that is safe from the cat of my heart.

The burning coal now points me towards, towards them, towards us.

Your question of who I am, Virginia?

Do you believe in soulmates? I believe in goodness more, evil not too far behind.

I ask you, which wave I am amidst these waves crashing in my lover's heart?

Who is my lover? Who is yours? Who but the command of liberated writing? Writing is the feminine within me and within you. It is rebellion for the sake of the song.

The whole world is a jungle. We'll make it the jungle of our rebellion.

I say: a woman in love is a crystal that reveals the spirit's secrets.

A sweet illusion that gifts you its rain and lightning and takes all your heartbeat in return.

The illusion of stones that I bring closer to my heart to give our ancestors the gift to contemplate the destruction of the universe. Stones carved to reveal water, while I remain thirsty.

Water is here but you drown while thirsty. Did death quench your thirst? Was it your eternal salvation?

Here with you, close to your river, we tell our stories. Our laughter rings out. Sometimes we cry.

Write what you believe, as long as you are capable of consistency with your idea, as long as you can make it bear fruit that heals wounds.

Writing is not merely letters and words. It is the meaning of life. It is the mirror in which we see ourselves as we are. Would a mirror lie?

Oh Virginia, your yellowed book carries your scent to me. It tells me about you and the depths of your readings.

The empty space before me now.

The mountain behind me and in my heart.

The ashes that struggle to conceal the ember of living. The living in the river that is weighed down by the question of stones.

Vera Maria

Die Kunst ist weiblich. Art is feminine.
Die Natur ist weiblich. Nature is feminine.
Die Armut ist auch weiblich. Poverty is also feminine in the language of my exile.
Whose femininity? Mine. Ours. The migrant women from our developing worlds. The woman who spends her life working fifteen hours a day is no stranger to me when, overcome by the weariness of questions, she takes a seat, as I do, on the underground train. Nor is the other passenger who pinches his nose against the odour of sweat and exhaustion sticking to her synthetic clothes. No soft cotton for her. The fabric of her life is woven from long threads of sorrow and short threads of happiness.
Poverty is a woman from the south of our earth. This is what the politics of manufactured oppression keep on the quiet in these borderless times, the times of the village-like world.
Der Gesang ist männlich. Song is masculine. How is it then that men wage wars?

* * *

On the subject of Earth and nature, her face lit up. Vera. Vera Maria is her name.
Vera was as delicate as the breeze. Or was the delicateness of the breeze borrowed from Vera?
She was a light breeze and a voice that split your suffering into two rivers, the sad Nile and the Danube, witness to the waltz of pain.
Vera and her flutes and an Ottoman rababa.
The instrument—no, it wasn't just an instrument, it was an eighteenth-century soul that woke up and spoke at Vera's touch. When Vera's fingers delicately tapped the Ottoman rababa, the longing of old tambour songs flowed from the far north of the heart's landscape and the echoes filled the place.
Tenderly the rababa told us: close your eyes all, dim the brightness of the noise within yourselves and soak up the murmurings of the earth. When I sing, close your eyes to the ugliness in the world

and open your hearts to the beauty within you.
So I did, along with everyone else.
Vera dedicated her second song to me and said that the outlook I shared earlier in the evening, when we exchanged stories about the earth, about women and art and my attempts to humanise politics, inspired her to sing the earth song for me. She said that I was a daughter of the earth.
I closed my eyes. I surrendered to the earth and felt my blood play symphonies through my body. Contact with the earth is the soul's elation at the highest point of its cosmic longing.
So be it. I and the earth and Vera's song are the story, the zenith of the kohl that adorns our mind's eye.

Antonia

Time is her story. Place is her story too.

Antonia plays music. I'm drawn by her strings as she plays her favourite instrument, the balalaika. Her blond hair is like a field of wheat hanging towards the sky. She puts down her white napkin and begins to pick the strings of her instrument. Every time I take this route, I watch her as she plays her story, the story of the Russian lands, of dreams of justice, socialism, and equality.

'I met him in Kazakhstan. He promised me a horizon to spread my dreams and my strings, to ferment my soul and plunge it in the sea of his love,' she starts to tell me her story, her eyes shining like the wheat fields adorning the land of my body, irrigated by loss. And then... and then language gets stuck in her throat.

I ask her permission before taking her white napkin, soaking it in water and wringing it out. I tell her in an attempt to explain, 'When I started, over sixteen years ago, to learn the language through which I experienced my exile, from within the language in which I felt human, it felt like wringing out this napkin for drops of water.' She laughs, her tunes filling her eyes with hope.

She begins from the place of nothingness and speaks with sadness. I ask her about her family. I want to find a way to walk with her through the gates of hope. Yearning for those faraway mountains. Her eyes light the darkness of my night, and the night before, when I lay in the ashes that resisted all attempts to wake the forgotten ember within.

She tells me that, as well as learning German, she is also studying art, with that old professor who rejuvenates himself with painting. She asks if I've met him, and I say, yes, I've just met him in your laughing eyes and one day I'm sure I'll meet him in person. She has waited for a long time, she says, to get a place to study the song of colours with him. Colours sing, it's the truth, and she likes to wait. Ich mag das Warten. I say, Das Warten ist das ewige Feuer.

She raises her left eyebrow, an arrow sharp enough to pierce the heart of a genuine lover, not the one who sold her to the mafia of human traffickers.

Ewige? Ewigkeit. She asks what it means, Ewigkeit? Then she

looks for it in her mini dictionary and doesn't find it. It means eternity, the kind that traps the souls of lovers. A word that has no place except in eternity itself.

Durst
Das blühende Schweigen
Dazwischen küsse ich deine Wolke
Wolke des ewigen Warten

I laugh at myself entering Goethe's den. She picks up her brush and begins to paint my words. The scribbles and spoils of the previous night when my fingers broke through the ashes and failed to wake the ember. Is this how fires die? No, it's not dead yet and I too like waiting. I translate what I said in German into Arabic.

Thirst
A blossoming silence
Meanwhile I kiss your cloud
The cloud of eternal waiting

She paints while I think of the waiting that tastes like thirst in my mouth. Antonia's story is that of thousands of girls who get sold in slaughterhouses of human flesh.

Mariem Hamoud,
translated by Nariman Youssef

My Father's Footsteps

I can tell my father's age by the way he walks. I remember, as a child, how I used to suffer when I went out with him. He walked so fast and took such wide strides; I could never keep up. When we got home, my mother would lecture him, saying he needed to be more considerate, and he would smile, a smile not unlike my own. Everyone comments on how alike we were, to which I always reply, 'I should be so lucky!'

As I got older, the distance between us diminished. Sometimes, he would be a metre or so ahead of me, other times I caught up. Then I took up running. Every day I ran for many kilometres. It might have started out as a desire to catch up with my father, or outdo him. I didn't know then that competing with one's parents would always end in loss. Children shouldn't race against their parents; when they do, they never catch up.

I'm still a runner. For years I've been waking up at dawn every day to race against myself. It has become a habit, and my stride has become wider and faster. The steps of a five-year-old don't measure up to those of a woman in her twenties. But the twenty-something doesn't measure up to her fifty-something father. Even when she's fifty herself, she's forever a five-year-old to him.

I go out with my father now and see that his legs aren't what they used to be. They seem to be cashing in on the strength and speed they gave him in the past, as extra rest and comfort. His walk tells me how he has aged. No one else would be able to tell by looking at him. But no one else remembers how he used to walk or suffered like me because of it. Sometimes, I feel like I've stolen his legs. If everyone agrees on how alike we are, could it be a coincidence that while his legs are no longer the same, mine have gained in strength and speed? Daughters steal their parents' legs, and mothers know all about that. My mother says that I resemble him, that my walk makes her think of him: another piece of evidence in case I had any doubt.

I walk beside him today without overtaking him, just letting him be a step or two ahead, but he knows my tricks, so he looks at me and smiles, and sometimes reaches for my hand to bring me closer, which of course I don't resist.

I walk beside him as he tells me about the day he left his camel and how my grandmother ran after the Land Cruiser that was carrying him across the Sahara. About the first dollar he earned in sub-Saharan Africa. About riding the longest train in the world, and about his happiness when he finally arrived in the Gulf.

I walk beside him, slowly, he and I beside the Gulf, under the sky of the land that we both love, our footsteps aligned. All I can think about is how he aged and how I too got older. We walk, neither of us overtaking the other. But I never doubt that he has been ahead of me since the day I was born.

My Father Died Twice

My mother said that my walk had changed since my father's funeral. She said that even if she were not my mother, she would have been able to tell that my father was dead from the way I walked. I believed her; she was exceptionally good at reading footsteps. She used to recognise people by the sound of their steps. She could tell what type of music they liked just by looking at how they walked. Sometimes, she could even tell someone's country of origin or ethnicity, just by watching them walk.

My father had asked to be cremated and for his ashes to be strewn in the Tigris. Twenty-three times, he repeated this wish. We used to sit around the table every morning. My mother's smile would fill her face, reflecting on all of ours, until my father would hold up his cup, half filled with tea, and chuckle as he said, 'Do not forget my words. My ashes belong to the Tigris. Take me back to the river when I die, yes?' My mother would rush us to finish our breakfast, as if in denial of what she must have known to be the truth: he was dying and keeping it from us.

He used to be the first one awake in the mornings, but had been sleeping in later and later. My mother and sister had begun to get up before he did. And when I too woke up to find him still asleep, I knew it was serious.

In the past, I used to hear him chastise my brothers: 'You missed the morning prayer! Shame on you, wallah what a shame!' I never heard him raise his voice except when it came to prayer times. In all other matters, I gauged his anger by how low his voice was. The lower his tone, the angrier he was. His silence had told us we were dealing with something grave.

For a week, I had woken up before he did. Then just as I was getting used to that, he had started to cough. On the first day, he had coughed for two minutes. On the second, for four. On the third day, his coughing fit had lasted for nine whole minutes. On the fourth day, he had opted for silence, then died.

I had heard my younger sister scream. I had been in bed, a pillow over my head and lifting my hand to press the snooze button, when my brother had pulled the pillow off me and said, 'Father is dead.' He had held my hand and sobbed.

I had stared at him, my father's last wish reverberating in my head: 'My ashes belong to the Tigris.'

Numerous arguments within the family had followed. One of my uncles had opposed my father's last wish, while my mother, another uncle and I, had insisted on carrying it through.

As the years went by, my father watched over me, as he had always done, now from his place in the glass jar on the shelf. Thick ashes. I hadn't made it to the Tigris yet, but his last wish was halfway realised. How time passed!

* * *

My mother was busy; she owned three textile shops and her inheritance from my father has enabled her to grow the business. But she made sure to come and see me that night, to give me her blessings before the trip. I was finally going to Iraq. My bags were packed and everything was ready. I asked the new cleaner to stop coming and told her that I would contact the service agency to ask for her by name when I got back. She seemed to know what she was doing. Plus, her cooking was delicious.

I greeted my mother at the door, then excused myself for a quick shower. When I came out, she was making dinner, and for the first time, I noticed that a few things were not in their usual places.

'This waste basket, didn't it use to be in the living room?' I asked her.

'How would I know?' she said. 'It's your home.'

Ah well, I thought, that was the downside of getting others to take care of your home for you.

We ate dinner and discussed many things. That night, it really hit me how my mother had aged. She mixed up events, even invented some. I just nodded and assured her that I remembered everything exactly as she recounted it. It hurt to see her like this, her mind no longer strong enough to hold all the memories in.

We finished eating and cleared the table together. As we left the kitchen, I was a few steps ahead of her when she said, 'Why has your walk changed again?'

I thought about it. The last time my walk had changed was when my father died, or so my mother had claimed. But why would it have changed again?

Then my mother asked, 'Where's the jar?'

I looked at the shelf in the living room and I didn't see it, so I looked back towards the kitchen. There he was, my father, the jar with his ashes, standing amidst the spices, almost used up.

His last wish was so close... *I* was so close to making it come true. I did everything to make sure I was.

The shame weighed on my eyelids. I had ruined everything. I couldn't see. I reached for my mother and couldn't find her. I tried to scream. I tried again.

Some time seemed to pass before I felt my mother's touch. I opened my eyes and saw her, a broken image of her. I couldn't grasp her properly. My right eye was broken and my left was blind.

'Where's my father?' I asked her.

She said nothing.

'My father, Mother. I must take him back to the river.'

Still Running

He had always been out of the ordinary. When he walked, it was never him walking down a road but the road taking him where he wanted to go, his shadow always a step ahead. His shadow was his armour, shielding him from the tragedy of time, safeguarding him against the abyss of the future. He was extremely cautious but that didn't help. He still woke up one day to find tragedy stuck to his face. He screamed and heard no sound. He screamed again and again but still no sound and to no avail.

Even when he was an average person, complaining about average things, no one understood him. So how would anyone understand him now, when his ailment could only be described as extraordinary?

He asked himself: was the earth so narrow that tragedy found nowhere to go but his face? Hiding inside him would have made more sense. Why then settle on the surface of his face?

He was fearful. And any speck of calm he had left was wiped away by the flood of questions that came at him. What's wrong with your face? You look strange today! Did you sleep okay last night? Have you missed breakfast today? Do you feel feverish? Who hit you?

He didn't want to hear their questions. He was fed up with lying and wished he could just tell them that the thing sitting heavily on his face was tragedy itself. But he was sure they would then unanimously declare him insane. He used cold water, hot water, added salt, scrubbed his face with a towel, tried to peel the tragedy off with his fingers. All to no avail.

He decided to forget about it, pretend it wasn't happening. He got dressed and went out, not knowing where he was headed. Hadn't the road always carried him? He stood outside the house, but the road wasn't moving. He took a couple of steps into the middle of the road and still nothing happened, except that he was almost hit by a car. Could it be that he had become ordinary?

He looked at his shadow and found it lying at the ordinary distance for the time of the morning. His shadow was no longer a step ahead! What a loss! His eyes brimmed with pain. He walked not knowing where to go, his very soul hurting. Again, he tried to scream, again to no avail.

Only a few seconds had passed before he heard a noise behind him, like someone running. He turned towards it and saw; his shadow running away. Before he knew it, he was running and yelling after it. To no avail!

He had forgotten that such things happened and were out of one's control. His shadow ran further and further away from him, the noise now gone, leaving no indication of distance or destination. It's the nature of things to take on a life of their own, so that they are no longer your business even if they once were.

He kept running. He is running still.

The Truth Is Not Enough

Sitting here among the books, I might as well be in Heaven. I write my reviews and end them all with the same line: 'considered fit for circulation'. The office runner is a nice guy. Every now and then he comes by to ask if I need anything. I answer no, because what could I possibly need while reading *The Land of Blackness* by Abdulrahman Munif? He goes away, then comes back with a cup of black Sulaimani tea and a smile. I thank him and return to Abdelrahman. It's beautiful here, everything seems fine to a horrifying degree.

Colleagues' voices reach me from beyond the door. Abdulmaali is the officer responsible for evaluating political books. I hear his cough and another colleague's laughter as someone jokes, 'Corona!'.

I'm in an office with two girls who love handbags. Dior ones, as a matter of fact.

'What's *your* favourite?' one of them asks me.

'I like tote bags,' I reply. She smiles, an abrupt smile, or maybe she doesn't smile at all. In any case, I don't think she and her friend like me much, but I try not to jump to conclusions.

The supervisor comes in every now and then to tell us that we need to hurry up with our tasks. He hasn't assigned anything to us; I or one of the others usually remind him. To this he has one response which he likes to repeat: 'In this work environment, you must always be getting things done, not waiting for assignments. Understood?' He leaves, and I dive back into *The Land of Blackness* while the other two go back to their monitors and discuss: which of these two handbags is prettier?

It's been a month since I started working here. Books are brought to us on a regular basis, a large number from all the publishing houses. Our job is to read them and determine their level of compatibility with publishing regulations, occasionally writing detailed reports.

The only feelings that compete with my joy at being here are shame and guilt. I know that I hold the fate of these books in my hands, that it's my duty to stand guard over them. I must fulfil this duty to the best of my abilities. The books are like dependents; I'm responsible for them. I read during my working hours, I read on my way home from work, and I read when I get to the hostel. The capital is a strange place. I used to spend at least every morning stuck in traffic at Maqta Bridge, but now I barely notice that I've left al-Ain before I find myself arriving in al-Mushrif. Occasionally, I take a longer route because Darwish is yet to get to the end of his poem.

Every morning on the way to work I mourn my losses. A hundred and forty kilometres are enough to cry over all that happened and all that didn't. Somewhere between Rimah and Khazna, my mother calls. She's never late, and I pray to God she never will be. As soon as I get to work, I start smiling. We all smile. The director says that we must leave our problems and sorrows at the gate. That's his way of spreading happiness among the department's employees. Nothing wrong with that. I like smiling.

I smile at Ahmad, the security guard, and he smiles back. I smile at Ruqqaya, the secretary, and she doesn't smile back. I smile at Khaled, my desk neighbour, and he looks suspicious. Every day for a month now, he has given me the same look. I can tell he doesn't trust me. More often than not, we rate the books as it pleases us. Everyone who works here knows that the truth is lost. It's the point at which all our endeavours converge on failure. We lie on occasion. The truth alone is not enough for us.

The office runner returns with bottles of water that he distributes around the desks and leaves. A little while later, Khaled has excused himself, but not before bringing my attention to the books waiting on his desk. I tell him that I'll take care of them. But it's strange that he's leaving now. It's only half past eleven, and we usually finish around two.

I dive back into *The Land of Blackness*. There's some noise outside. When I look up, the two girls are not at their desks. The noise is getting louder. I'm about to go check but then remember the books on Khaled's desk and busy myself entering them into the system. There are two books that he has marked as 'unfit for circulation'—I put them aside on my desk to look through later. The noise keeps getting louder. I enter the details of the last book and stand up. I look at the time: 11:47. There's no one in the corridor. I go to the office next door and find no one there either. The noise has stopped and all of the rooms are deserted. I head for the stairs, look down into the stairwell and see no one. I run down the stairs. Again, no one. I leave the building and stand in the car park, empty except for my car.

Ahmed Isselmou,
translated by Sawad Hussain

Floating Paper

Though I'm standing three feet from the shore, the bitter cold waves slap against my feet. I feel for my small backpack, pulling the straps closer to me, hoping to feel some of the heat it absorbed from the sputtering taxi engine, its rumbling still echoing through the sand dunes.

Everyone around me seems preoccupied: a thirty-something woman rocking her baby, murmuring words I can't make out; a black man distracting himself with his pile of cigarette butts; a boy building huts out of moist sand, using his foot as the foundation. He builds them again each time they are washed away. A wheatish young man taking on the sea by writing in the sand. I steal a look, trying to make sense of his nervous letters, but the overlapping squiggles make me give up. It's a language that I was never taught.

The whole scene reeks of monotony. I'm desperate to talk to someone I can trust. The atmosphere of emptiness is overwhelming. A tinge of sadness veils the sky that seems displeased with what I'm doing. Angry thunder rumbles from afar and featherweight clouds roil up from the depths of the sea, rushing to gather far from the prying eyes of those in their lavish homes in the capital.

Little by little, the bag loses its heat. I feel the urge to reorganise it, even though I have spent over three hours choosing what deserved to come along: a small Hisn Al-Muslim booklet, a miswak chewing twig of soft arak that I had to trim for it to fit, a key to an old Chinese lock, a Bic pen, a bunch of papers from one of my weathered notebooks, a pair of fitted jeans, and other random things, meaningless things, I don't know why I chose them. That's when I see it, the photo.

Eagerly, I pull it towards me, as if seeing it for the first time. Rough hands over the years have left it creased. It's Mariem, leaning back against a sidr tree, her fingers tightly interlaced, her hands cupped around her right knee in a rare state of contemplation. Traces of henna stain the fingernails of her tapered fingers, her milhafa wrapped tightly over her head—I still don't know the colour of her hair—then pools elegantly over her arms, masking the rest of her figure. At a distance behind her stands a palm tree, its date clusters drooping down heavily. Soft strands of the setting sun make their way between the sidr and the palm tree.

It's difficult to make out any colours in the black and white photo. But if I am to hazard a guess, then her milhafa is light blue, dotted with white, purple, and navy. Her moon-like face radiates, her nose slightly upturned, haughtily. Her wide eyes find refuge beneath her lush lashes and arched eyebrows. Her dark lips form a mysterious Mona Lisa smile, intersecting at an undefined point with her confident gaze. All this makes whoever is scrutinizing the picture think that Mariem wants to divulge a secret that she has kept buried for years on end.

In the lower right-hand corner, the date of when the photo was taken—over ten years ago. A bad habit now common among older photographers, taking the fun out of choosing the date that you want. People always want to pick dates for their memories, whatever they end up being, dates that suit them in the here and now.

When he raises his arm, the sleeve of the black man's winter tunic falls slightly, revealing an old digital watch. 'It's been three hours,' he mumbles in broken French, as he kicks an empty water bottle into the air. It lands next to the boy insistent on building his huts.

The wheatish man waves his shirt either to alert or call for help, and everyone rushes towards a dinghy, on its side something in a foreign language that I come to understand later: *Dreams Come True* in Spanish, intersecting with *Bismillah* poorly written ingreen. The sound of the engine is grating. Lips move in unison, to the same rhythm...

Three feet from the shore, a rectangular, white piece of paper is tossed by the waves and ends up by the remains of the boy's sand creation. From its creases, I can tell it's the photo of Mariem.

'Stop! Stop! Please!' I call out.

The woman's spittle flies while she tenderly buries the child's head in her bosom. The black man's stirring voice sings out, flooding the boat with a sense of spirituality.

The piece of paper disappears on the horizon.

Hamidinou's Smile

Hamidinou is a popular figure in Mauritanian folklore, one who is referred to as a symbol for laughing off hardships when it hits from all angles. The story goes that Hamidnou is captured by his enemies and, as his head is laid on the chopping block, starts laughing. When asked why, he replies, "Right now my wife thinks I'm not with her because I'm with another woman."

Carefully, he read the handwritten notice in the bank window: PLEASE COUNT YOUR MONEY BEFORE YOU LEAVE. Yes, it was all there: seven thousand. Exactly what the teller had said his balance was.

He looked at his phone: 10:10 am. *No worries, I've still got more than enough time* he told himself. *She'll probably be an hour late anyways.* His head swam with questions, while he made sure to put his weathered wallet in his shirt pocket. He fastened his jacket zipper. It wasn't cold, just a safety measure he had learned living on the streets of Nouakchott.

He squeezed himself in with five other passengers in a car that barely stopped by the intersection east of Marche Capitale downtown. His trouser pocket vibrated. The passenger crammed next to him on his right felt it too. With great difficulty, his hand found a way to his phone. He didn't get to it in time, but it had been her. When he tried to call back, it was the usual, 'Sorry… you have run out of credit.' It won't be that way for long, he reassured himself.

Upon reaching his destination in the far-flung suburb Toujounine, in the most eastern tip of Nouakchott, he was the only one left in the rickety car. Impatience was clear on the driver's face.

'Turn left here please!' he barely managed to get out.

'You've come all this way for one hundred,' the driver exploded. 'And now you're asking me to turn? Five times the diesel price has gone up this year, but I get paid the same?'

He tried to come across as compassionate, 'But if you do turn left and wait ten minutes for me, I'll ride back with you to the Madrid intersection, and pay you four hundred. What do you say?'

The driver didn't respond but stopped nonetheless in front of the laundry shop that the passenger pointed out.

'Your clothes aren't ready. Now don't you complain because you haven't paid a single ouguiya since…' was the laundryman's greeting, preoccupied as he was with gathering a pile of dirty clothes.

'I'll give you what you want, but I need my clothes now. I've got somewhere to be and I need the right clothes.'

The brawny laundryman winked at him. 'Well, if that's the case, then you really don't have anything suitable. Have a look at those clothes piled up on the table over there. The owners aren't in a rush. You can pay me 1500 for the daraa, wear it to where you need to be and then return it tomorrow.'

Again, his pocket vibrated. The sound was distorted but he understood, '"Call me back, I'm out of credit."'

That reminded him that he too, was out of credit. He went to get some from the man sitting under the umbrella at the front of the shop, and gave him 1000 to charge his phone with 1500. On his way back to the laundry, the grouchy taxi driver had since gotten out and started yelling, 'Since you're not in a hurry, just give me my money. Stay here till Judgment Day for all I care!'

'Please, just a minute.'

'No time.'

Ignoring the driver, he strode to the table and chose a white, beautifully embroidered daraa, then turned to ask, 'Isn't there a sirwal to go with it?'

'Trousers are over there, but you'll pay another 500.'

'Let's settle that later,' he said, turning over the trousers to choose a pair that suited the daraa. But the laundryman's vice-like grip was enough to make him understand. 'Okay, like you said, I'll give you 2000 for the daraa and sirwal, and tomorrow when I return them, I'll pay the rest.'

The laundryman's grip on his hand slackened a bit but he didn't say a word. He simply took the 2000 and then busied himself with collecting clothes strewn around the shop. As he was stepping out, the laundryman said something he couldn't hear completely because the taxi's horn was blaring in one long sound, but knew it

had something to do with the police because he heard 'shurta'.
His phone vibrated once more, but then stopped. He called the number back, getting an earful. He stayed quiet. Calmly he answered, 'Look, azizati, the trip from Casablanca to Nouakchott takes two and a half hours. I've still got plenty of time.'

'But I don't want to see anyone before you in the airport,' said the girl that he had a thing with, the one he had never seen other than in a photo.

'You won't see anyone before me... but how can I be sure it's you? I'll be wearing a white daraa and a blue shirt, carrying a board with your name on it.'

'*My name?* Do you hear yourself? My family will be waiting for me and if one of them sees my name on a board in your hand, you'll spend the night at the police station. You'll be able to pick me out. Let your heart guide you.'

His phone chimed in his ear letting him know that his credit was nearly out. He hurried to finish the call. 'What counts is that I'll be there before you come out. Take care of yourself.' But she didn't hear his last words.

For the tenth time, the taxi stopped, but this time at the Madrid intersection. He handed the driver 500 and alighted, waiting for his 100 change, but the driver said haughtily, 'Been waiting for you for more than ten minutes, this hundred is for me.' He slammed the door in response and the taxi rattled away as fast as it could.

When he crossed the road, he remembered that he had been carrying a daraa and sirwal, that he had paid 2000 ouguida for. He turned back, but the car had melted into the traffic; in its place, a large truck shuttling more coal sacks then it could hold.

Shouting at the top of his lungs, he tried to stop the taxi, but the looks from pedestrians and passengers in cars, and the horns of those in a rush, confounded him. He rushed to a parked taxi and panted, 'Follow that car, I left something—costs more than 50,000.'

'And how much will you pay me?' the driver said coldly.

'Whatever you want, just catch it!'

'Well, I can't guarantee that, but sure, get in. Do you know where it's headed?'
'Marche Capitale.'
'Souq! Souq! Souq!' the driver yelled.
'What are you doing? I told you the driver went that—'
'Are you paying for six passengers?'
'Fine, but let's go now.'
The traffic was suffocating. Thirty minutes passed before they even reached halfway. The driver turned right, asking, 'Do you know his name, or the license plate number?'
'Of course not. If I did, I would have called my friend at the police station and not be paying you 600 ouguiya.'
After ten minutes the car stopped at the intersection on the east side of Marche Capitale. He searched drivers' faces stuck in traffic, maybe he'd find the one he was looking for, but his current driver prodded him, 'Pay me my 600, and take the rest of *your* day finding a needle in the haystack.'
He paid him 1000, and took his change, while scrutinizing the faces along the road. His eyes fell on a car parked in front of an open-air shed where women were dyeing clothes. One of them gave a paper to a man in a hurry who slammed his taxi door. He tried to stop him by yelling but the driver spotted him in his broken side mirror and took off like a shot on a dirt path between the buildings. He tried to get the license plate, but it didn't have one.
He asked the store owner if she knew the man, and before she could respond, he added, 'This daraa and sirwal are mine.' He told her the whole story, but from her face it seemed that this woman twisting her miswak flossing stick didn't understand what he was saying. She did say that the prices for dyeing differed based on the type of clothes and the intensity of colour.
In vain, he tried to make her see. Making his way to a heap of clothes, he picked out the neatly folded daraa and sirwal. 'These are mine.'
'But they belong to the driver who just left,' she protested.
'Do you know his name or his phone number?'
'No, I don't.'

Gritting his teeth, he took his phone out from his pocket to call Ibrahim, his police friend. But the screen was dark—the battery, dead. Deep inside the pit he had fallen into, he decided to return to Toujounine. The watch on the wrist of the passenger wedged between two others said it was five past two. It occurred to him to stop at the Madrid intersection in the middle of town, nearby to some relatives of his that his friend Ibrahim often visited. At least he could charge his phone there.

Parched beyond reason, he bought a cold juice from the nearby grocer and paid 200 for it. Another 100 went to the phone credit seller.

When he entered his relatives' house, their fifty-something mother smiled at him saying, 'Our troubles are over! Here's Ahmed. Thank you, grandfather, for coming through for us and answering our prayers!'

Taken aback by what she was saying, he said, 'What's wrong?' before even greeting her.

'It's Fatima. The pain in her stomach is unbearable. I think it's her appendix. We've got to take her to the hospital.'

'But I don't have a car.'

'I know, but you must find us one. Just look at her.'

He looked at the young woman doubled over in pain, and remembered what affection there had been between them, before she married her cousin who migrated last year to Spain, only to send a notice of divorce in the post and 10,000 ouguiya after the birth of their child.

'Okay, okay. Just put my phone on the charger till I catch a taxi.'

'I'll also need 2000 from you to take us to the end of the month, I don't have enough to buy her medicine.'

He didn't answer, his head spinning with the daraa and the sirwal.

* * *

With his jacket atop his head, protecting him from the blazing sun, he tried to weave through those departing the mosque. But one of them yanked the jacket off his head.

'Aha! Even if you hide your face, I can pick you out of a crowd of a thousand men!' He turned to try to see who was speaking, but the man barely gave him the chance. 'Didn't you tell me that you'd pay at least 2000 today? Do you think the Internet is free? Up every night till sunrise with that whore, and you don't want to pay.'

'Say that again. I'll punch your face in. She's more honourable than you.'

'If she's so honourable she wouldn't be up with you every night when she doesn't even know you.'

'It's none of your business.'

'Give me what you promised, I've got an electricity bill that I've got to pay today.'

'Take this thousand and the other thousand I'll give you soon.'

'Hah! Not a chance. You know you actually owe me four thousand. And I've been so patient with you this whole time.'

'I've got some exceptional circumstances. Fatima needs an operation…' he mumbled, slipping away, but the man's voice reached him, something about calling the police.

He brought a taxi to his relative's home and paid the driver 400 to take Fatima and her mother to the hospital. Closing the car door, she called out to him, 'And what about when I get there?'

'All I've got is this,' he said, handing her a 1000 note from his wallet. Only 100 left.

'May Allah bless you,' she said, clasping the note while his ringtone led him back inside the house. He flipped open his outdated phone without looking at the number. 'Where are you?' an intimidating voice growled.

He took a moment to look at the number and saw it was the laundryman. 'What do you want?'

'I want the daraa that you have on you right now, the owner is standing on my head. One whole hour, I've been trying to get a hold of you.'

'My phone was off…but…'

'No buts. If the daraa isn't back here in an hour, you can only blame yourself.'

Somebody else's voice, tense, started to speak before the call was cut off. He tried to call back, but the all-too-familiar message rang in his ears, 'Sorry. You have run out of...'
'Unbelievable. I just put money on this.'
'Mama used it before she left,' a young girl sucking her thumb said.
'Who did she call?'
'Mohammed in Ivory Coast. She said there wasn't enough money and threw it back there.'

* * *

With his jacket on his head, he walked for ten minutes and then waited for another ten in the back of a rundown car alongside three other passengers, waiting for it to fill up before it left for Toujounine.

A police car stood in front of the laundry shop and a hand gestured to him. Before he could even lift the jacket from his head, a heavy blow came down on his cheek and another paw crashed down on his head. He was thrown in the back of the car.

* * *

A fashionable young woman dragged a classy leather case behind her, after leaving the passport-stamping window. Her father's embrace enveloped her; her father, who had been waiting for her next to immigration, smoking a premium cigar. Right outside the arrivals exit, a four-wheel drive swallowed her up. She searched the bright faces and furrowed brows of those waiting to receive their loved ones, glancing at the photo on her phone to remember what he looked like, but the car windows were too dark for her to make out much...

* * *

At the police station, the portly investigator sucked greedily on a cigarette as he asked for his name. Dabbing at the blood on his lower lip, he smiled and said, 'Hamidinou.'

Batoul Mahjoub,
translated by Nariman Youssef

Extract from *Minefields*

Past midnight on a cold October night. Sleep just out of reach. I drag my feet to the kitchen to pour myself some muattaq tea, no sugar. Back in my bedroom I sip it with the kind of bliss only an after-hours cup of hot tea on a cold night can bring. The pale pages are scattered before me; their paleness making my insomnia even worse. I pick up the first page. Some words have been blacked out. I try to delve into what lies between the whiteness of the blank spaces and the blackness of what's been omitted. It feels like a betrayal of earlier drafts. What is she hiding behind those crossed-out words?

My fingertips touch the ink, trying to wipe it off, but all I feel is the cold. I nestle myself in a corner of the room, away from the ice-like walls, and pull the blankets all the way up to my runny nose, curled up like a cat. My eyes rest again on Mariam's papers and I reach for the blazing ink of her words. Before long, I have forgotten the chill in my limbs and let the blankets, one after the other, fall away from my body. The fire of the words is enough to diffuse the cold. The pain in them is almost audible.

Of course, I have only myself to blame; did I really need this additional dose of pain? Why did I open the mystery envelope José brought me? Couldn't I have drifted off to sleep with a Fairuz song, crooning about the quietness of the night, like girls dreaming about a better tomorrow would do? I'm lying to myself. I can't help but be tormented by Mariam's secret papers that hold in their grip the secret of the desert.

I'll let her tell me then, on this October night, about the desert…

* * *

Skin the colour of wine, captivating sharp features. Brutal on cold nights and delightful on moonlit summer evenings. The desert locks her secrets in her chest and walks tall. Her stories are epics.

This is a land pregnant with the stories of the men, women, and children I used to know, and still do. The truth of who they are is written on their faces. Their deep complexion highlights their features, which are open with joy despite the harshness of the desert and its changeable seasons. Do you think you know them as well as I do, José? Why do you not answer me? Has the question crushed your tongue? Or is it the fear of delving into their stories? What are you cautioning me against? Stirring things up; all those stories loaded with pain and suffering, with minefields and walls? Are you afraid of stepping into the sand wall mined with explosives?

Be quiet, Mariam. Please. Be quiet. What wall are you talking about? Don't you know that the walls have ears?

I will not be quiet. How could I? Can you not hear the screams and groans of those who lost their limbs? I will not be quiet. Do you not know that there is a wall? Have you not heard about the minefields? What are you scared of speaking about? Let me speak then: about the landmine victims, and the share of pain that I carry. You do not know them like I do.

I look at you in silence and let you speak. You've always been fearless and foolhardy. Now you risk yourself to speak about the victims of a wall of sand and landmines. Be careful; the walls can hear us.

You only warn me because you're ignorant about me and about the victims' pain. I come from the land of deep-brown shades. The people I belong to walk on burning earth, victims of a wall of sand and long stretches of landmines, a berm of death that rules over their footsteps, and intercepts anyone who dares to cross from here or there. Have you ever seen a landmine? Do you even know what one looks like?

No, enough. I don't want to see it or know it.

Anti-personnel mines. Do you know what they are? Or what they are made of? Let me tell you: Anti-personnel mines are triggered when someone steps on them. According to Wikipedia, mines manufactured after the 1950s generally use plastic casings to hinder detection by electronic mine detectors. Under the flat surface of the casing is a spring-loaded striker that, when pressed or stepped on, sets off a detonator with highly sensitive explosives and poisonous pellets. Sometimes a mere vibration of the ground nearby activates the detonator. Some mines become more dangerous with the passage of time. Have you ever seen a landmine as I did? You haven't, have you? I saw it lie in wait one misty morning, preying on innocent souls as young as roses, on the wise souls of elders, and the graceful souls of the women of my homeland. I saw the torn limbs of my compatriots fly with the shrapnel. Landmines stop everyone crossing from one side to the other. And the roar of landmines breeds anxiety in every heart. Every small joy could turn without warning into a hefty sorrow. My story is a story of minefields, destructive to strangers and kin alike. José, don't ever dare to cross the desert without a guide. You could find yourself face to face with the wall, or in the danger zone where explosions threaten on both sides.

I would walk through a desert of landmines with you, for you. Have you forgotten that I'm the one who worships the deep shades of that North African land? Mariam, tell me, do you think of yourself as Arab?

My belonging lies with the whole of humanity.

What you are, mi amor, is my volatile love story.

* * *

I have never forgotten how his warm whispers awakened a heart worn out by absence, how his hot breath awakened dormant desires in the hidden nooks of my spirit and my body, even as we stood not far from the wall of sand and landmines and close to watchful eyes of strangers and kin who registered every move.

My memory escapes back to the day I boarded a ship headed for a western coast, with landmine victims seeking treatment and psychological rehabilitation. I still remember the travellers' faces. And how I almost forgot all the pain of landmines when we entered the open water, intoxicated by the sea and the rocking movement of the waves. I was on the top deck, enjoying the open expanse of the water and sipping my evening coffee, when I noticed a man trying to get my attention. His accent told me he was Spanish, probably one of the rehabilitators working with the group. Not feeling like talking, I ignored him, discouraged him with a dismissive look. The sea alone was enough to console me and heal my wounds. I remember being cruel, indifferent, and mocking, which really went against my nature. What was happening to me? Why was I blaming this innocent Spaniard for the landmines' crimes? How was any of it his fault? Especially when he had crossed the sea to treat our wounds? But then again, what good was dressing wounds?

The next day, looking out on the ocean with my morning coffee, I had forgotten about wounds and landmines and my amputated arm, but I was still thinking about the look in the man's eyes which I had so easily dismissed the night before. I shut myself up in my cabin until we docked at a western port. My host, a brother from back home, took me to my hotel where I thanked him for receiving me so well. I spent the next few hours busy preparing my paper on the horrors I had witnessed, on the planters of death in the desert.

I travelled from one city to the next on an awareness-raising campaign. Throughout, the man's lingering gaze stayed with me. I blamed myself for pushing him away. Why had I not given him a chance, just to talk? And why was I still blaming myself for a mere glance that I had ignored on a passing evening? Anyway, by the time I had returned to the Sahara, I had forgotten the captivating green of those eyes and stopped blaming myself for ignoring them.

Fast-forward many years. I was visiting another country where the threat of landmines was rampant. I had been there for several days, running an awareness campaign and taking part in a conference, when a man who looked about fifty approached me. With a gentle smile, he asked about the landmine victims in the Sahara and their rehabilitation. It surprised me to run into someone who seemed informed about landmine victims in my homeland. What else did he know about the Sahara, about its history? At the end of the conference, he asked me out for a coffee. We talked and talked, and all the while I looked at him closely. The look in his eyes felt familiar and his features weren't strangers to my memory. Where had you seen him before, Mariam? I tried to remember. Of course, this fifty-something man with the grey sideburns was none other but the young man who accompanied the landmine victims on the boat all those years ago.

I never forgot how you rejected me that evening on the boat. How come you're being nice to me now? What has changed?

We smiled at each other then. Without my having to answer your question. We both knew that time was all it took to change us.

We may accidentally fall in love with someone who no longer inhabits our memory. Years may stand between us before a reunion that comes like an evening dream. We find each other with greying hair, tired faces, aching hearts. Could love make up for all that has been lost?

The memory makes my heart ache. My heart had failed to forget you. Was the warmth of your voice all I needed to face the desert wall to protest against the planters of the landmines. Was your whispering voice what I needed to keep me in touch with myself? You smiled and carried on talking, as if you were listening to my secret thoughts.

You won't stop me from venturing into the desert and crossing the minefields with you, or from exploring the captivating mysteries of the Sahara in your company.

* * *

Writing this on a cold evening in October, wrapped in the black cloak of night, I stir a sugar cube in the bottom of a cup in a corner of a forgotten café by the border, with the echo of your voice for company. Your voice that rose in anger against the bloodsuckers and harbingers of death, the dawn visitors, and late-night arrests—it cuts through the clutter of memories: No more! No more landmines! We want love, we want peace! No more landmines!

* * *

We stood by the wall of sand and landmines. On my right, sharp-eyed Ali—brown skin, features earnest beyond his years, a real patriot in love with his country—stood tall with his shotgun on his shoulder. Every time I complained about the sight of the weapon, he joked that the gun makes the man. Women fall in love with brave men and brave men carry guns, he said. But you know how I hate war and blood, Ali. I'm a woman in love with peace.

Then there was Ahmad with the nom de guerre, from the Eastern Levant, handsome face and eyes as green as springtime in el-Sham. He comes from Kessab, has Armenian roots, carries in his heart the pain of historical trauma. Seeing him brought the scent of Levantine history soaked in Damascene jasmine. Ahmad, the peace-loving Armenian fighter, came to the mythical Sahara in search of peace. How long would he last under its burning sun?

There was also Omar, in his thirties, with unruly hair and olive skin, a son of the Sahara who had immigrated one scorching summer day in search of peace and work in a surrogate homeland, away from the minefields. But none of the cold exiles were enough to compensate for the warm embrace of his sunny birthplace. He returned for the sun that only rises in the country whose features he shares. But his mother had departed to heaven while grieving his absence. He returned to find an icy homeland in the absence of her warm embrace and wept as he remembered the morning he had left without saying goodbye.

And Michel, the elegant Frenchman from Nice, an adventurer who loves to explore the desert and delve into its geography. The day he got here, he decided to learn the language of the Sahara, live in tents, make his bed on the earth with the stars in the sky as his blanket.

On my left was Yusuf, or José, in his fifties, his roots grown out of Saharawi origins—that's what his Spanish mother told him about the father he never met.

What was to be done with an Andalus that had nothing left of our ancestors' glories but historical ruins that mourn in silence as they stand still before the tourists' cameras.

The Andalus was widowed before her time, Mariam. You know what? The Andalus is like Wallada bint al-Mustakfi waiting for her poet lover to come back and wipe her tears.

José raised his voice to the faces of the planters of death, chanting in delicious Spanish:
Basta basta!
Basta de mina anti personas, queremos amor, queremos paz!
Basta de minas!
His fist was raised in place of mine, the warmth of his arm around me a consolation for my missing arm, the one I had lost one dark morning as the homeland of my pain helplessly watched. No more! We want love, we want peace! No more landmines!

* * *

Mariam's voice echoed her anger and rose alongside José's, Ali's, Ahmad's, Omar's and Michel's, as they all marched along with many others to protest against the landmines planted in this African land. No more landmines! Enough death, enough destruction! We want love, we want peace!

I gather Mariam's papers, scattered on my bed, and reorder them in the envelope that José gave me on that rainy morning. There are the accounts of minefields and landmine victims, which kept Mariam awake at night and brought almost as much suffering to José, who was in love with Mariam and the Sahara.

I pause before their correspondence—filled with love, yes, but also obsessed by the victims of minefields, arrests, and forced disappearances. Countless stories carried in the folds of Mariam's and José's private messages. Do I send these to the publisher, along with everything else?

Arthur Gabriel Yak,
translated by Sawad Hussain

Divorce

Foreboding tension tinged with the smell of bodies and the tobacco smoke that he was puffing out of his hairy chest, with visible irritation, charged the sky of the sitting room. He was straining to thread together the stray ends of their chatter, hanging in the air like dust motes; he was trying to unravel the spell of the choked atmosphere. She, his wife, was surrounded by a halo of disbelief that their marriage, five decades long, was now a decrepit building on the verge of collapsing. All the efforts of family and friends were akin to merely tossing a rope at a shipwreck, buffeted by the waves, hoping to save one person, at least one.

She felt her bulging eyeballs brim with an acidity that almost set off the volcano of rage behind her spectacles, their lenses as large as the bottom of an empty cup. Suddenly, without warning, she saw herself swimming in the current of a beautiful dream, drowning in the details of bygone years as if it had all happened yesterday. She saw her six children, now married with their own homes. The eldest had been just two, playing with mud and sand, her caked hands dirtying her muddy hair even further. As she left behind whatever she was playing with, she knocked down with her leg—unintentionally—a clay kitten that she had fashioned with her tender fingertips, then fled from the neighbour's dog which came out. It licked her face with great affection.

On that evening, she had laughed a lot, the sun tumbling towards sunset, her husband chuckling along with her after the children had gone to bed. They started to inhale the scent of each other's breath, tasting the drops of their saliva seasoned with the spices of love. The night was a beautiful, sweet-tasting woman celebrating their love that didn't feel the fatigue of strenuous intercourse; rather, they tasted a sweet, gratifying tiredness, tickling every cell in their bodies. Afterwards, they relaxed and surrendered to the army of somnolence that invaded their castle of wakefulness, allowing them to fall into a slumber of a dream caught between reality and imagination.

Indeed, she felt all this, sitting in that living room, now a dog-eared matchbox— or was it a solitary confinement cell? He, an exile crowded with family and friends trying to discourage him from the decision that plunged them into a maze of confusion. She stared at his face for a long time, as he smoked one cigarette after the other, his face creased from stubbornness and having drowned in a sea of fresh love. She contemplated him, scrutinizing his face. Had she ever really known him? She couldn't remember where they met, their first look, their first kiss. All those firsts had melted away, like a lump of ice, dripping between the letters of that word that thumped her head like a boulder fallen from a mountaintop. She saw that word, loathsome as it was, stinking like a school toilet bowl, sneaking out from the pages of the dictionary in her mind, bidding farewell to the other words, and, after a lengthy embrace, poured out from the pages tearfully, telling them, 'I'd rather die than remain a prisoner to these yellowed, dirty pages, smeared with thousands of fingerprints.' Lamenting, the word rolled out, leaving the dictionary without looking back, and began to roam about the room, only to settle in the mouth of her husband, filled with the flavour of tobacco and love, a word that haughtily settled there.

He gathered his belongings, soul broken, eyes wandering, refusing to meet her gaze.

Just like that, after fifty years of marriage, he left the house, never to return.

After sitting unmoving for hours, she got up, standing on legs that might as well have been brittle twigs. Crouching down, she reached for the dictionary and flipped through it, looking for the word that had rolled out, swum and nestled in her husband's mouth. All the other words were where they should be, except one which wasn't on the page of its entry. She felt compassion for her husband who had been covering up the holes of his new life; compassion tinged with hatred, love, delirium, and revulsion when she learnt that the word was nothing other than... Divorce!

* * *

Things hurtled ahead with the speed of a shot. He had married a girl fifty years his junior. He was now spending his honeymoon in one of the coastal cities looking out at the Indian Ocean. More and more were coming to light. A week later, she found out that he had left this world before his honeymoon was even up.

She wanted to scream, she wanted to laugh, she wanted to cry her eyes out. She wanted to undo the ring of the knell from her mind.

She wanted, and she wanted, and she wanted. But in the early evening of that fateful day, she was there, lying down next to her husband in the All Saints cemetery.

A God and His People

The king convinced his hapless subjects, who worshipped him blindly, to the point of death, that his throne was in danger and a sacrifice was necessary to save both the kingdom and the people from perishing.

For his people, the king was the divine incarnate, to be obeyed and worshiped more than The Creator Himself.

They didn't waver, holding him up as sacred, and knelt before him, not hesitating for even a moment, before granting his wish. Like a deluge they streamed forth, unconcerned by anything other than stamping out the threat to the pillars of the kingdom. There they were: children, women, old and young, throwing themselves in the face of peril to save the kingdom.

The people died by suicide. The kingdom survived.

Heartened, the king sat on his throne, intoxicated by the smell of blood, charged by a life of plenty, indulging in the luxury of his ever-growing power day after day.

'The king's only happy when his people are dead!' an old woman cried out, seeing the people rush towards their death with such lamentable enthusiasm.

The next day the king felt his heart hollow: he no longer enjoyed the taste of his authority, his eyes no longer satisfied with his piles of wealth and status, his hungry body no longer sated by the beauty of his maidservants. His crushing appetite was only appeased by the spilling of more blood, the wrecking of more souls. He called for more people to assemble while he perspired, anxious how they would respond this time. He convinced them that the royal family was in danger, that a large disaster was looming, the kingdom and its people in the crosshairs.

The subjects looked towards the four corners of the kingdom, but failed to see the imminent danger, or any disaster that would wipe them out. But, in their innocence and ignorance, in their blind love for the one seated on the throne, responded to the revered deity's demand. Each one killed themselves to protect the kingdom, the king, and the royal family. The kingdom fell into a vicious cycle: deception, trust, suicide, followed by more sacrifices for the sake of the divine king.

On a beautiful, sunny morning, where colourful wings ornamented the sky, and starlings warbled their harmonious melodies, the king woke up, his heart heavy, his mind perturbed and his soul thirsty. His burning thirst would only be extinguished by his people; their blood for his throne.

As was his custom, he called on his people to quench his thirst and ease his anxiety, but to his surprise, there was no one left to sacrifice. They had all laid down their lives for his illusory battles.

And that was how the king lost his throne and his power. For where were his subjects?

Mama Regina's Cruel Blessing

Flabby, fleshy bodies press down on my ribcage, smothering my frantic cries, exciting them even more, like some sort of sexual pick-me-up or a bitter winter's chill that makes street dogs chase bitches all night long.

Their different-sized things tear apart the walls of my small space down there, experimenting from one style to the next, squashed in that room: the oppressive priest style, the smell of their drunken mouths sucking all the air out of me, to the street-dog style, where I feel as if my insides are going to pass through my mouth. They all like lying down on the old faded table that Mama Regina bought second-hand, on her way back from Mass one day. Sometimes, it is the game of standing up in the open-air bathroom, the summer sun beating down, high in the sky, tearful, looking down at me, heartbroken.

I feel as if the city's sewers are emptying their filth into my torn-up insides.

* * *

Before I came here, school was all I thought about. My teacher made me fall in love with those strange shapes, letters: together they were words and sentences and had meaning; a wonderful world on paper. My tall and slender teacher, dragged away by a soldier during the Great Chaos, disappearing with her into the thick grasses that surrounded our village. She screamed. Ten minutes later, we heard gunshots and her voice melt into the sky above.

In my village, everything was beautiful and tasted sweet.

My brother and sister had been making dolls out of clay, gently touching brilliant butterflies with their soft fingertips, while the drizzle left drops on our lips and cleansed our souls. The memory sticks in my mind.

Now, there are no raindrops on my lips or breeze to cool them. Sorry if I tell you that they, here, in the big city that I used to hear about, they wet my lips, against my will, with their veiny things addicted to making their way inside, and the thick liquid that follows afterwards, full of disease.

Don't ask me about my sister who had been licking the hardened snot right above her upper lip. Don't ask me about my younger brother, his ribs poking out. All I can say is the machine called a Kalashnikov harvested them.

Yes, the both of them. Mama and Baba too.

I was twelve years old when the madness of the city swallowed me. Running away from my village that was nothing more than ashes.

How is someone like me, without family, supposed to live in the capital?

Do you blame me for doing it with them to survive?

I learnt everything here. Everything, in Gumbo-Sherikat; call the neighbourhood what you like, it's all the same to me. Here, I learnt that I was a child cut off from her roots by the horrors of war, something a twenty-year-old girl blessed with living in her parents' embrace would never know.

* * *

The rain stopped pouring down when the evening began to scatter the kernels of darkness into the universe. It was then that I saw her whispering with a foreign truck driver, the one I had seen just an hour ago. He had been gulping down booze, clearly an alcoholic for many years, blowing out smoke from his cigarette outside a small bar without much light, near the main road leading to Nimule. He nodded at me. I ran away from him, my heartbeats almost reaching home before me. Mama Regina asked why I had been running, and I told her.

We used to call her Mama. And why not? Didn't a generous person like her deserve such a title, taking in a stranger like me and other young girls?

Mama Regina cackled when I told her why I had sprinted back here. She patted my shoulder warmly. 'Don't worry. That man, he's good like me. He'll never hurt you.'

They were whispering in her room when the night laid out its shadows. Sleep took me by surprise while the autumn breeze caressed my body.

When Rania and her sister Rita—names that I later learnt had been made up by Mama Regina—fell into a sweet sleep, I saw the outline of Mama Regina standing at the door, gesturing at me to follow her. I fell in step behind her, easily led, crossing the small space that separated her room from ours, what might as well have been a mud hut. The sky was sorrowful, in its bosom small stars glittering faintly. We entered her clean room smelling of sweet perfumes. There, we found him, sitting on a wooden chair, next to Mama Regina's bed, half of a lit cigarette dangling from his lips; he took a drag and exhaled, without his hand ever touching it. I could only see half of his face in the candlelight, but I knew it was him, the alcoholic from outside the bar. I froze.

'It's really very easy,' Mama Regina whispered. 'Just a piece of flesh will go inside you and make its way through. The world will still be as it is, beautiful. Nothing will change, not one little bit.'

She came to me with flowery soap and ordered me to bathe, to change my filthy dress for a new, soft see-through skirt that she had pulled out from the corner of her cupboard. Then she sprayed me with perfume, as if I were a bride, and left the room to us, the room swimming in a cloud of acacia wood incense, drowning really, in Bint El Sudan and Fleur D'amour perfume.

The skirt revealed my womanly parts, exciting him even further; he stuck out his tongue and licked his lips, taking one drag after the other of his second-rate cigarette. I don't know how many times the foreign truck driver did it to me, his mouth reeking of tobacco, alcohol, and snuff. Nasty beads of sweat dripping from his armpits and his neck. But when I woke, the morning sun was streaming through and my entire body ached. The sight of blood smeared across my skin made my skin crawl.

My legs shook, unable to carry my body. Mama Regina came to me all smiles, speaking to me with an over-the-top joy about how I had become a young woman oozing magnetic femininity, able to satisfy her visitors' desires and make their fantasies come true. Now I could pay for my room and board. She said I could buy the clothes and perfumes that I liked, even get my hair done, or get a weave, all from my own money, in any of the fancy hairdressers.

The most horrible things in this world happen with the snap of a finger, so easily, most people can't even wrap their heads around it.

You think when you first come to the big city, that you'll be able to get so much out of it. Not a chance! The city, at least for me, took so much. Left me naked.

* * *

I used to do it every day, just as Mama Regina wished. Even so, not a single time did I have what I was told was an orgasm, or a 'gunpowder explosion of pleasure' as one of the more experienced girls put it. Sexual drives too furious for a slim, girl-like body like mine.

I used to receive the strangest types—me, a product in low stock but high demand. Soldiers in combat uniform, cleaners dragging behind them the fatigue of backbreaking work, on their way home from having thrown out the city's trash in open plots, only for my turn to come for them to empty out their own filth inside me. Salesmen roaming with their second-hand Chinese goods, tossing them into dark stalls in the Gumbo-Sherikat souk, rushing to Mama Regina's house to extinguish their burning desires, and young men whose shining bodies smelled of privilege, they too, not hesitating to…

All of them, every single one, their saliva would pool and run over my curves.

Mama Regina, who would tuck the money that I earned for her into her push-up bra, between her saggy breasts with their wrinkled nipples, was happier than my mother the day she welcomed me into this world. From my money, which Mama Regina took most of, I had to buy make-up, whitening creams, hair removal creams—to make sure I was as smooth and white as could be. I was a manhood magnet, as she put it, and all this would bring in more money. There was never enough to cover all my needs but I always made sure to buy condoms even though none of them ever used it, saying that the plastic got in the way of the thrill.

Disaster almost struck when one of them took out a gun and placed the mouth to my temple. He removed my clothes and my bra and … he was happy, overjoyed really, softly humming a catchy tune when he emptied the contents of his hard member.

Another guy doubled the usual rate because, as he said, he wanted to feel pleasure crawling like ants on the sides of his uncircumcised man bit. Apparently, he knew all about Quranic verses.

'Nothing shall ever happen to us,' he said, 'except what Allah has ordained.'

* * *

I no longer felt anything, I no longer smelled the rot in their mouths, I no longer felt any pain.

It seemed that my small opening down there had loosened, meaning their things would float in without rubbing up against the pleasure-making walls, and so they grew to hate me. Mama Regina no longer bothered with me, no longer chose me to please her customers. I was exhausted all the time, wasting away, everyone could see it. I would be tired when they did it to me, so she pushed me to the side—Regina, that is—to the sides of her business, making way for Josefina, the thirteen-year-old girl, who had come knocking one rainy night.

Josefina was beautiful, fresh, charged with a femininity that the fishmonger forced open. A man who, phone in hand, hurried to the souq and came back with pounds to place into Mama Regina's outstretched palm. Howling and shrieking, the kind that comes from someone who has just received the news of death, ripped through the quiet wall of the evening. An evening wrapped in clouds, that surrounded the moon with a gloomy, grey halo. We found Josefina lying face down, trembling, whimpering like a wet cat.

Mama Regina ordered us to leave the room at once.

The fishmonger was sitting in a corner, puffing away, gloating, in a cloud of his local tobacco. He smiled at Regina who raised her right thumb at him as if to say, 'Bravo'. She then started to pat, with exaggerated affection, Josefina's shoulder, whose head was thrown in her lap.

The fish seller was the first to violate Josefina, a child—just as he violated the lives of fish every day—all thanks to Regina's plotting. She counted the notes and stuffed them in her bra, a large smile of satisfaction on her face, as always, whenever a young girl was stained with the blood of her virginity and she—Regina—received a wad of cash in return.

* * *

I wasted away. Worn out more than usual one evening, Regina came to me with some porridge and scooped up a large spoonful to pop into my mouth, all the while looking at me very suspiciously. I had already thrown up twice before sunset that day. The number of clients coming in was less than what we had on other nights.

'Bitch, you're no longer any good to me,' Regina roared in my face. She said I was carrying a bastard.

Suddenly, my mother's image flooded me; she held my younger brother and sister by the hand. They wore the clothes that people are buried in. I was happy to see them coming towards me. I got up and quickly walked to meet them mid-way. We met next to a grave that looked like the dome of a dilapidated church; I stretched out my hand and smiled at them. They were looking into the space of a distant journey.

Your family died after the 15th of December. This isn't your family! a voice within me cried. My hair stood on end and my skirt was drenched in sweat. I tried to yell but it came out as a weak hiss, as if I were an old snake. At the top of my voice, I yelled out this time, and saw Regina standing above my head. My legs were heavy with drugs. A woman in her thirties stood next to Regina, and uttered words that I caught the edges of. '…more than four months.' Then she whispered upon feeling the movement in my body, 'It's murder, breaking the law. It's a human in there, and she could die too.'

'What law! How many people were killed last year?' spat Regina.

Josefina came to me crying after they both left, with another girl in tow, one I didn't know. She must be the fresh catch. I learnt from Josefina that I was going to be thrown out.

It was a dark night and the sting in my stomach got stronger at the start of each hour. Josefina stayed seated next to me. Regina was busy with her clients in the usual evening get-together at the end of the week, not concerned about my shining stomach, round like a hot air balloon. The pain started to spread its armies, while the needle pricks were now in every part of my body.

At midnight the sacrificial girl that Regina had brought, whose hand she had just held shortly before, let out a yell. I shrieked loudly. Not out of sympathy with the poor girl but because the pain between my thighs was extreme, as if there were two cars tied with chains, one to my right leg, one to my left, and driving in opposite directions. This was the pain I was in when I heard his cry; him sucking on his white fingers.

I smiled, and Josefina did too. She blew in the air, a kiss, for my child sucking at my nipple.

When I raised my head next, I saw her standing, her hands on her waist at the door to the room, her eyes flashing, irritated. Josefina fidgeted on the edge of the bed, and I cleared my throat. His lips smacked loudly as he sucked at my breast, annoying Regina even more.

'You and your bastard child better not be here tomorrow,' she seethed. 'I saved you from the war, and this is how you repay me?' Her nasty words rang in my ears as she turned and walked away.

* * *

Ever since I ran away from my village when the war broke out, and lost my family, things didn't stay the way I knew them to be. I was no longer that innocent girl; I had become the mother to a bastard, just as Regina said.

Josefina gave me some fish soup to drink and I fell into a deep sleep that I only woke up from the next day. Rather than waking up on my own, Josefina's screaming that did it for me. Regina was sitting on the edge of the bed, staring at me with a look filled with a mix of sympathy, gloating, and what I understood to be doubt.

I didn't see my baby next to me.

I searched for him under the sheet and between the two pillows I had propped behind him yesterday to stop him from falling. I gave her a hard look but she kept her eyes elsewhere. She murmured, then mumbled, then wringing her hands, stammered, 'Your son is dead.'

'But I had heard his cry; felt him at my right breast, where he had clung last night.' The words came out of my mouth, bitter and hoarse. The sound that came out of me was like my child's cry. I put my hand on my cheek, and looked to see if it was Regina sitting next to me or the pure evil that was within her. Without thinking I dug my fingernails into her neck and yelled, 'My son! Where is he, Regina?'

She sat cold, quiet, extremely still, as though she didn't feel my fingernails tainted with her filthy blood. After my waves of anger grew calm, she hugged me hard to her chest. I smelled the overwhelming scent of motherhood rising from her smooth armpits, and with the edge of her short dress, revealing her branched veiny on her thighs, she dried my tears.

I took in a deep breath. My chest shook as the air came out of my lungs in short bursts. Regina took a deep breath too and said, 'It's better this way.'

'My son is dead and it's better this way?'

She grew quiet, staring into space, then rose and walked towards the door. As she stepped out, she said, 'Can't you see? Now you can *finally* get back to your work!'

The door slammed behind her and the echo of that slam repeated in the cracks of the walls of the crumbling room and the ceiling of my cracked head. At that moment, I realised that it was the echo of a solitary prison cell, one that I had chosen to live in, chained, weighed down by Mama Regina's cruel blessing.

Contributors

Najwa Binshatwan (from Libya and residing in Italy) is an academic and novelist, and the first Libyan to ever be shortlisted for the International Prize of Arabic Fiction (2017). She has authored three novels: *Waber Al Ahssina (The Horses' Hair)*, *Madmum Burtuqali (Orange Content)*, and *Zareeb Al-Abeed (The Slave Yards)*, in addition to several collections of short stories and plays. She was chosen as one of the thirty-nine best Arab authors under the age of forty by Hay Festival's Beirut39 project in 2009.

Dr. Ishraga Mustafa Hamid (from Sudan and residing in Austria) holds a PhD in Political Sciences from Vienna University, as well as a Masters in Communication Sciences. Her activism concentrates on culture and the arts, specifically from a perspective of gender and diversity. Her passion is to connect people, especially women activists. She has published eight books in Arabic and German, including her autobiographies, prose, lyrics, and reflections on life in Sudan and Austria. She has also translated nine books. Dr. Hamid has received several prizes in Austria and globally, such as the Extraordinary Ambassador for Gratis Culture (FCG) in Beirut. In 2020, she received The Golden Medal of Merit from the Republic of Austria.

Mariem Hamoud (from Mauritania and residing in the United Arab Emirates) is a short story writer. She has published several short stories among various newspapers and magazines, garnering several prizes. In October 2019, her first story collection, *He's Still Running,* was published. She combines literature, language, and media, and is interested in the arts and different methods of human expression.

Sawad Hussain is an Arabic translator and litterateur who is passionate about bringing narratives from the African continent to wider audiences. She was co-editor of the Arabic-English portion of the award-winning Oxford Arabic Dictionary (2014). Her translations have been recognised by English PEN, the Anglo-Omani Society and the Palestine Book Awards, among others. She has run workshops introducing translation to students and adults under the auspices of Shadow Heroes, Africa Writes and Shubbak Festival. She has forthcoming translations from Fitzcarraldo Editions, MacLehose Press, and Restless Books. She holds an MA in Modern Arabic Literature from SOAS. Her Twitter handle is @sawadhussain.

Ahmed Isselmou (from Mauritania and residing in Qatar) is a writer and journalist. He has several published works including: *Waiting for the Past* (a short story collection published with Arabic Scientific Publishers), his first novel, *Perforated Life* (published with Dar Al-Shuruq), and his most recent novel, *The Outsider*, which will be released soon by Dar Al-Adab. Yale University choose one of his short stories, *The Runaway Decade*, to be included in their Arabic curriculum. His short story, *Floating Paper* (included in this collection), won a 2009 competition organised by BBC Arabic. Ahmed works as a news bulletin editor for Al Jazeera news channel.

Batoul Mahjoub (from Southern Morocco) holds a BA in Arabic Studies and a Masters in Communication and Discourse Analysis, both from Ibn Tofail University in Morocco. She is currently a PhD student researcher. Her publications include: *A Man's Elegy* (2007), *Dark Days* (2011), *Southern Wrench* (2014), *Minefields* (2016), and *Dune Ladies* (2019).

Garen Torikian is a fiction writer, essayist, and translator from Western Armenian into English. A recent graduate of the Masters in Literary Translation at the University of East Anglia, he is currently an MFA candidate in Fiction at Columbia University. Follow him **@gjtorikian**.

Arthur Gabriel Yak (from South Sudan and residing in the USA) is graduate of Cairo University in Egypt. His published works in Arabic include: *It Doesn't Matter You're From There, A Day Azrael Committed Suicide, Soprano of the Resurrection*, and *Gabo Dances Flamenco and Tango*. He has also translated a YA novel into English called, *The Beautiful Humble Bird*, authored by Stella Gaetano.

Nariman Youssef is a Cairo-born, London-based, semi-freelance translator working between Arabic and English. She holds an MA in Translation Studies from the University of Edinburgh, part-time manages a translation team at the British Library, and runs and curates translation workshops with Shadow Heroes. Literary translations include Inaam Kachachi's *The American Granddaughter*, Donia Kamal's *Cigarette No. 7*, contributions in *Words Without Borders, The Common, Banipal*, and poetry anthologies *Beirut39* and *The Hundred Years' War*. Follow her **@nariology**.

Acknowledgments

Many thanks to **Anna Brewster** for her tireless work designing this book, **Polly Halladay** for her editorial insights, **Jen McDerra** for her wise counsel, **Molly Beale** and **Erin Maniatopoulou** for their deep camaraderie, and **Danyel Madrid** for her never-ending encouragements.